The Mexican Americans

LINDA R. WADE

MAJOR AMERICAN IMMIGRATION

MASON CREST PUBLISHERS • PHILADELPHIA

Dozens of Mexicans wait for the sun to set near the border in Tijuana. Once night falls, they will try to complete their trek through the desert and enter the United States.

The Mexican Americans

LINDA R. WADE

MAJOR AMERICAN IMMIGRATION

MASON CREST PUBLISHERS • PHILADELPHIA

Mason Crest Publishers
370 Reed Road
Broomall PA 19008
www.masoncrest.com

First printing

1 3 5 7 9 8 6 4 2

Library of Congress Cataloging-in-Publication Data

Wade, Linda R.
  The Mexican Americans / Linda R. Wade.
      p. cm. — (Major American immigration)
  Includes index.
  ISBN 978-1-4222-0614-0 (hardcover)
  ISBN 978-1-4222-0681-2 (pbk.)
  1. Mexican Americans—History—Juvenile literature. 2. Mexican
Americans—Social conditions—Juvenile literature. 3. Immigrants—
United States—History—Juvenile literature. 4. Mexico—Emigration
and immigration—History—Juvenile literature. 5. United States—
Emigration and immigration—History—Juvenile literature. I. Title.
  E184.M5M666 2008
  973'.046872—dc22
                                                2008026013

Table of Contents

MAJOR AMERICAN IMMIGRATION

America's Ethnic Heritage

Barry Moreno, librarian

Statue of Liberty/

Ellis Island National Monument

Ethnic diversity is one of the most striking characteristics of the American identity. In the United States the Bureau of the Census officially recognizes 122 different ethnic groups. North America's population had grown by leaps and bounds, starting with the American Indian tribes and nations—the continent's original people—and increasing with the arrival of the European colonial migrants who came to these shores during the 16th and 17th centuries. Since then, millions of immigrants have come to America from every corner of the world.

But the passage of generations and the great distance of America from the "Old World"—Europe, Africa, and Asia—has in some cases separated immigrant peoples from their roots. The struggle to succeed in America made it easy to forget past traditions. Further, the American spirit of freedom, individualism, and equality gave Americans a perspective quite different from the view of life shared by residents of the Old World.

Immigrants of the 19th and 20th centuries recognized this at once. Many tried to "Americanize" themselves by tossing away their peasant clothes and dressing American-style even before reaching their new homes in the cities or the countryside of America. It was not so easy to become part of America's culture, however. For many immigrants, learning English was quite a hurdle. In fact, most older immigrants clung to the old ways, preferring to speak their native languages and follow their familiar customs and traditions. This was easy to do when ethnic neighborhoods abounded in large North American cities like New York, Montreal, Philadelphia, Chicago, Toronto, Boston, Cleveland, St. Louis, New Orleans and San Francisco. In rural areas, farm families—many of them Scandinavian, German, or Czech—established their own tightly knit communities. Thus foreign languages and dialects, religious beliefs, Old World customs, and certain class distinctions flourished.

The most striking changes occurred among the children of immigrants, whose hopes and dreams were different from those of their parents. They began breaking away from the Old World customs, perhaps as a reaction to the embarrassment of being labeled "foreigner." They badly wanted to be Americans, and assimilated more easily than their parents and grandparents. They learned to speak English without a foreign accent, to dress and act like other Americans. The assimilation of the children of immigrants was encouraged by social contact—games, schools, jobs, and military service—which further broke down the barriers between immigrant groups and hastened the process of Americanization. Along the way, many family traditions were lost or abandoned.

Today, the pride that Americans have in their ethnic roots is one of the abiding strengths of both the United States and Canada. It shows that the theory which called America a "melting pot" of the world's people was never really true. The thought that a single "American" would emerge from the combination of these peoples has never happened, for Americans have grown more reluctant than ever before to forget the struggles of their ethnic forefathers. The growth of cultural studies and genealogical research indicates that Americans are anxious not to entirely lose this identity, whether it is English, French, Chinese, African, Mexican, or some other group. There is an interest in tracing back the family line as far as records or memory will take them. In a sense, this has made Americans a divided people; proud to be Americans, but proud also of their ethnic roots.

As a result, many Americans have welcomed a new identity, that of the hyphenated American. This unique description has grown in usage over the years and continues to grow as more Americans recognize the importance of family heritage. In the end, this is an appreciation of America's great cultural heritage and its richness of its variety.

1 New Life in a New Country

Pantaleon Ochoa was born in Mexico in 1904. As a child, he heard the stories of how his family had left Spain and moved to Mexico many years earlier. As Pantaleon grew up, his family suffered because they were poor. There was no work for them. They had to live in a one-room shack.

When Pantaleon was about 19, he decided to strike out on his own. He, too, would migrate. He was going to go north to the United States.

He went with some friends to Encinal, Texas. Encinal was a little town between San Antonio and Laredo. Only about 300 people lived in the area, but they had crops that needed picking. Pantaleon found work in the cotton and onion fields. He also met a young lady named Paublita Martinez. She had been born in Mexico and moved north as a young girl. Pantaleon and Paublita were married in 1925.

Life was difficult for the young couple. They worked hard, only to earn a few cents. The Texas sun scorched the workers as they picked the crops. There was no cool place to go. Working in the fields could also be dangerous. Sidewinders and rattlesnakes hid in any available shade. Scorpions often darted away, but they were hard to see. Sometimes the workers would step on them and get a painful sting. Bobcats and coyotes were also around. To be safe, houses were built on top of tree trunks to keep the unwanted creatures out.

Even with these problems, however, Pantaleon and Paublita felt good about living in the United States. They were thankful for their fieldwork. Their family began to grow. In time, Pantaleon and Paublita became the parents of 10 children. Ricardo Martinez Ochoa (later called Richard) was the youngest of their ten children. He was born in Encinal on December 27, 1946.

The house had no running water and no electricity. Ricardo could see daylight through the cracks in the walls. His parents bought water in 50-gallon barrels. He took his baths in a big galvanized tub.

In time, Pantaleon returned to Mexico. Richard's oldest brother, Albert, joined the army. His second-oldest brother, Pantaleon Jr., (called Junior) went north.

Junior joined other migrant workers in the tomato and potato fields of Indiana. Then he moved to Michigan, where he picked cucumbers. He also met the lady who would become his wife. They moved Junior's mother and his brothers and sisters to Fort Wayne, Indiana.

Richard was only six years old at this time, and he could not speak English. A year later, his mother took him to a Catholic school where an interpreter helped Richard. He did so well in school that halfway through the first grade he was moved to the second grade.

A Mexican-American family sits outside their house in Texas. Many Mexicans start their life in America with small houses and few possessions.

Richard loved school. He enjoyed learning, but he didn't have a lot of friends. By the time he reached the seventh grade, he felt very alone. Then Richard went to high school. He became involved in drama and acted in some of the school plays. He also took a *drafting* class and

This letter was written in 1989 by a Mexican-American woman named Lydia Casarez. She is writing about the living conditions in a migrant camp:

This year everything really changed for our people. When we had to be over there in tomatoes we used to have to stand in line to get a shower after we came in from work. And over here every trailer had its own facilities. So they were real happy about the housing. In other years when we'd come in from work, it would be seven o'clock and we would still be in the shower line at ten thirty or eleven at night. This year nobody had that problem. Everybody was in their own house with their own showers.

discovered that this was something he enjoyed. His teachers encouraged him in this direction. His work was good enough that he found a part-time drafting job in downtown Fort Wayne. Now he was able to help his mother financially.

After high school, Richard joined the U.S. Army. He became a draftsman and served in Europe. While he was gone, two of his brothers went into the restaurant business. They bought a place and turned it into the first Mexican restaurant in the city.

After his time in the Army, Richard returned to his drafting job. He also worked part-time in the restaurant with his brothers. He was so ambitious that he even became involved with the Civic Theater. He acted in several successful plays, but it was his acting in a play called "The Boys From Syracuse" that gained the attention of the Julliard

School of Music. His picture was in the newspaper and on television. Then the business where Richard worked as a draftsman closed. Richard decided that he had to work full-time at the restaurant.

Today, Richard is still in the restaurant business. His delicious food lures not only Mexican Americans to dine at La Margarita but also many other customers who enjoy Mexican food. ✳

This brown and white patterned prairie rattlesnake is found throughout North America. The possibility of facing a snake or scorpion is higher in the unpopulated desert of northern Mexico, making attempts to illegally cross the border into the United States all the more dangerous.

Mexico is a beautiful country. It is a land of many contrasts. There are high mountains and lush green *plateaus*. In the northwest are deserts where the land is dry and hot. In the south, you will find a thick rainforest. A tropical forest is also part of the Yucatán peninsula.

Most of the middle part of the country consists of the Central Plateau. It extends from the United States border to south of Mexico City. Most of the major cities are in this area. It is also where many of the large farms are found. The weather is warm and provides a good growing season for crops.

The Mexican flag flies near the Zocola Cathedral in Mexico City. Mexico city is one of the largest metropolitan areas in the world, with more than 20 million inhabitants. Although Mexico is a beautiful country, its history of political and economic turmoil has forced many people to move north to the United States.

The tourist business is a major source of employment for people in Mexico. Visitors come from all over the world to visit coastal towns like Acapulco and Puerto Vallarta, located on the western coast. Beautiful beaches invite them to swim and play in the surf.

Mining provides work for many Mexicans. Mexico is rich in natural resources. Some of the world's richest silver mines are near

Guanajuato. Important minerals such as sulfur, lead, zinc, coal, uranium, iron ore, gold, and copper are also found throughout the country.

At first glance, it would appear that Mexico is a perfect place to live. But that is not the case in many parts of the country. Despite the richness of the land, there are simply not enough jobs in Mexico to provide work for all the people. Also, in the past the government has been unstable. This has been another reason why people have emigrated from Mexico, both legally and illegally.

During the 19th century, the United States and Mexico fought over territory several times. In the 1820s and 1830s, the government of Mexico gave a group of Americans permission to settle in the region that today is the state of Texas. At the time, this was part of northern Mexico. In 1835, these settlers decided they wanted to be free of Mexican rule. Their rebellion suffered a dramatic loss at the battle of the Alamo in March 1836. Six weeks later, Texan soldiers commanded by Sam Houston routed the Mexican army at the battle of San Jacinto and won their freedom.

The Texans established their own country, the Republic of Texas, which lasted for nine years. In 1845 Texas became part of the United States. The Mexican government was angry, because it had never officially recognized the independence of Texas. To further complicate the situation, the United States wanted to expand into southwestern regions controlled by Mexico. President James K. Polk offered to buy the land north of the Río Grande River in the fall of 1845. The

Porfirio Diaz had a profound impact on Mexico, ruling as president from 1876 to 1880 and 1884 to 1911. His period of influence is referred to as the "Porfiriato."

Mexican government refused.

When fighting broke out on the border, President Polk convinced Congress to declare war on Mexico in 1846. The Mexican army was no match for the Americans. By February 1848 the war was over. Mexico had

Emiliano Zapata led a band of rebels in the Mexican Revolution during the early part of the 20th century. A group of Mexican revolutionaries called the Zapatistas have continued Zapata's fight for the common people of Mexico.

to give up the territory that Polk had originally asked to buy. It included the present-day states of California, Nevada, and Utah, and parts of Arizona, Colorado, and New Mexico. The United States paid Mexico $15 million for this territory. This became known as the Mexican Cession.

In 1853, the Gadsden Purchase added more land to the United States. This land was the southern strip of Arizona and New Mexico.

The border between the United States and Mexico has not changed since that time.

The 75,000 Mexicans living in that area were given the choice of citizenship. They could be citizens of Mexico or the United States. Many of them chose to remain on their lands, and became U.S. citizens. Over the next 50 years, other Mexicans immigrated to the United States for various reasons. Some wanted to work in the gold and silver mines of California, Nevada, and other areas. Others came to escape poverty or to make new lives for themselves in the United States.

The Mexican Revolution of 1910 is an important point in the history of Mexican immigration. Porfirio Díaz, a *mestizo* general, ruled the country in the late 19th century and early 20th century. Under his

Mexico City is the capital and cultural center of Mexico. It is the largest city in the world. Over 20 million people live close together in the city, and it is hard to find work.

This is an old city with an interesting history. The Aztec Indians built the city (then called Tenochititlán) in A.D. 1325. During the 1500s, Spanish invaders destroyed the Aztec capital and built a new city on the ruins. That is present-day Mexico City. You can still see many of these Aztec ruins. You can also visit some of the beautiful palaces that were built during the Spanish colonial times.

rule the country's economy improved. Railroads were built, mines and oil wells were developed, and manufacturing factories were expanded. However, industrial wages were kept low. Attempts by workers to form labor unions were crushed. Native American communities lost their land to big landowners. Most of the Mexicans were purposely kept in poverty and ignorance. Big landowners gained more land and became richer. Only these landowners, businessmen, and foreign investors were able to live in nice homes.

In the election of 1910, Francisco I. Madero, a *liberal* landowner, ran against Díaz. Many people wanted Madero to win, so Díaz put him in jail. As a result, Díaz won. When Madero was released from jail, he left the county.

When Madero returned, he found that nothing had improved. He told the people that the only way to bring about change was through a *revolution*. Many of the people chose to follow him rather than continue to live in poverty.

Madero and his revolutionaries defeated the federal troops. They destroyed railroads and attacked towns and estates. Finally, in May 1911, Díaz left office and Madero became the new president. Madero had so much *opposition*, however, that he could not hold the country together. He was captured and shot by General Victoriano Huerta in 1913. The next year, Venustiano Carranza, a state governor, overturned the government again. Years of unrest followed. It was not until the late 1920s and 1930s that the strong revolutionary movement in Mexico finally faded.

General Francisco "Pancho" Villa was a hero of the Mexican Revolution. Villa aided Francisco Madero's successful over-throw of Porfirio Díaz's regime.

THE ROBIN HOODS OF MEXICO

Francisco "Pancho" Villa was a rebel general from the northern state of Chihuahua. He and a band of men rode about the countryside terrorizing rich landowners.

During the early 20th century Pancho combined forces with another rebel leader named Emiliano Zapata. Zapata was an Native American, and his main goal was to gain land for his people. Together, these men fought for the poor Indian farmers whose land had been taken away from them by the large landowners. Zapata's battle cry, "Land and Liberty," expressed the aims of their revolution.

Even after the revolution, Pancho Villa went on bandit raids. During one attack on Columbus, New Mexico, his men killed 16 Americans. President Woodrow Wilson sent General John J. Pershing into Mexico after him, but Pershing's troops failed to capture Villa.

Emiliano Zapata was killed in 1919. Pancho Villa was killed in Texas in 1923. Legend says that they protected the poor and terrorized the rich. Tales about their adventures are still told in Mexico today.

During this time, Mexicans were moving north to the U.S. They were afraid of the bandits who roamed the countryside. They wanted a better life for themselves and their families. But there were drawbacks. Most of them did not speak English. Many had no special skills. Large numbers of these people came from poor, rural areas and had never lived in a city. Also, many of these immigrants planned to return to Mexico after they had made enough money to start over in their homeland.

In 1917, the United States entered World War I. Now more jobs than ever before were available to immigrants. Farms and ranches needed workers to produce food for the armed services. Jobs were available in factories to make guns, ammunition, and clothing.

In California, there was a great agricultural industry. There were jobs available for everyone. Acres of land were devoted to the growth of fruits and vegetables. The laborers migrated from area to area to pick the ripe crops. By working the crop circuit, they were able to work almost all year long—simply moving from farm to farm, working in the fields.

This was hard for the families of Mexican immigrants, however. They did not have a permanent home. The children went from school to school. It was not uncommon for a person to work from sunrise to sunset for as little as 12 cents a day.

New mothers took little time off work when their babies were born. Two or three days after birth, they would strap their newborn into a backpack and return to the fields to work. The death rate for children was very high.

Often, Mexican men went across the southern border of the United States to find work. They usually went to New Mexico, Arizona, California, or Texas because they could go back home quickly. Immigrants from Europe and other faraway places did not have that option. For them, leaving their native country often meant never seeing their families again. This was not the case for the Mexican immigrant. Often the workers, or **braceros**, could come for the crop season and then return to Mexico.

The need for more workers increased when the United States entered World War II in 1941. Mexicans rushed in to fill more jobs. They had always been needed in the agricultural business. Now there were jobs in the shipyards and in aircraft and ammunition factories as well. Many Mexicans hurried to enter the United States and take advantage of these opportunities.

Immigration authorities in the United States did not know what to do about this population explosion. Some feared that after the war was over, there might not be enough jobs or places to live if these people stayed in the United States. This made the U.S. government seek a workable solution. The United States and Mexican government officials finally signed an agreement saying that farm workers could come for the crop season only. They would then have to return to Mexico. Some Mexican workers were given ***green cards***. They had to live on the Mexican side of the border and return to their own homes at night.

While many Mexicans became braceros and green-card holders, others entered the United States illegally. They crossed the Río Grande River at night. These people were called by the derogatory term "wetbacks." Others crossed the border at places in the desert where there were no patrols. At least two million Mexicans entered the United States illegally during this time. Immigration authorities were aware that Mexicans were entering the United States illegally, but since factories and ranches needed workers for the war effort, little was done to stop them from coming.

Life changed after World War II ended. Factories no longer needed people to build war equipment. American soldiers returned home from the battlefields of Europe and the Pacific and wanted their former jobs back. New jobs became hard to find, and wages went down. Mexicans continued to come to the United States, and job competition grew fierce.

Border patrol officers tried to keep illegal immigrants out. However, the border between the United States and Mexico is long, and many people were able to sneak across at night. Then they would hide

This Mexican man tried to hide in the upholstery of a van while friends tried to smuggle him across the California border into the United States. Border patrol officials say that tricks like this are common.

A group of Mexicans make their way toward the border as they prepare to illegally enter the United States from Agua Prieta, Mexico. Beside the dangers of the desert, illegal immigrants face possible confrontations with Arizona ranchers, who have been known to hold undocumented immigrants at gunpoint. Also, if U.S. border patrols catch Mexicans attempting to illegally cross into the United States, they will arrest the immigrants and turn them over to Mexican authorities.

in the **barrios** with Mexican Americans who protected and took care of them.

Illegal border crossings do not always have a happy ending. When Mexicans do not have the proper papers, they have to take whatever job is available. They are subject to arrest and **detention** for illegal entry. In 2007, the United States Border Patrol arrested nearly a million people attempting to enter the United States illegally. Many of them were from Mexico or Central America. That figure was actually down 24 percent from 2006. It is impossible to tell how many Mexicans have crossed illegally and were never caught.

Stories are told of how Mexicans have crossed the border. One illegal Mexican immigrant says that when he came over in the late 1980s, "it was as simple as crossing a street." He just waited in Tijuana, a Mexican city on the border, until nightfall. Then he climbed a fence into California.

During the 1990s, however, the United States Border Patrol put an end to easy crossings. The immigrants now had to cut trails through the hot desert, avoiding snakes and scorpions. They have even crawled through sewage pipes and dodged gun-toting **vigilantes** to find work in the United States. Despite the great danger, these people are determined to find a better life for themselves and their families. ✳

3 Cesar Chavez, Champion of the Mexican Worker

Although unions had been formed in the 19th century, these unions protected American workers, ensuring they got fair pay and proper working conditions. There were no unions set up for Mexican Americans.

Cesar Chavez saw the need for his people to be protected. He had been born in 1927 on a small farm in Yuma, Arizona. Cesar's father lost his farm during the Depression in the 1930s, and the family became migrant workers. Cesar was only 10 years old.

For Cesar, school was always temporary. He attended 30 different schools because his family was always on the move. He wanted to learn, but only got through the sixth grade.

Cesar grew up knowing *discrimination*. Sometimes, he could not go into certain restaurants. In the theater, he had to sit in a section specifically for Mexican Americans. He became angry and wanted to do something to help his people. Cesar

As president of the United Farm Workers of America, Cesar Chavez pushed for the rights of Mexican workers and farmers. He founded the National Farm Workers Association in 1962, and made fair treatment of Mexican laborers his life's work.

volunteered to work for the Community Service Organization. Sometimes he helped Mexican Americans get driver's licenses. Other times, he helped the people fill out legal papers. He also helped with voter registration and citizenship classes.

By 1962, unions were popping up even in small businesses. Mexican Americans began to show an interest in organizing a labor union. This was what Chavez had been waiting for. He formed the National Farm Workers Association (NFWA).

Cesar traveled and talked to the migrant workers. He found that the average pay was only $1.15 an hour. The migrant workers had to live in chicken houses and tumbledown shacks, with no electricity, running water, or indoor plumbing.

Cesar Chavez **rallied** the migrant workers together to form a union. As a union official, he took a California employer to court for paying less than the minimum wage of $125 a month and won. Then the union sued the Tulare County Housing Authority for better living quarters for the migrant workers. They won again. Tulare officials built modern accommodations for the workers.

Still, many employers did not pay well or provide adequate housing for their Mexican workers. Chavez felt the only way to help all the workers was to go on strike against the table-grape growers of California. The migrant workers refused to pick the grapes. Many went around the country asking people not to buy grapes. It was difficult to keep the strike going, but people sent money to the union to help the workers survive.

A Mexican migrant worker harvests tobacco leaves in Kentucky. For many immigrants, migrant labor is their only chance of securing a steady job, although it is grueling work.

Labor rights leader Cesar Chavez and civil rights leader Coretta Scott King hold signs at the head of a group of marchers during a protest in New York City. Chavez organized boycotts to rally for new employee contracts for labor workers and to increase the money they were paid by farm owners.

One time, Cesar Chavez was talking to students at the University of California. He told them, "If you want to help, don't eat lunch today. Hungry workers need your money." Several thousand dollars were collected that day.

The table-grape strike lasted about five years. Even mediators from the California Department of Labor failed to settle the dispute. Finally, a five-man committee of Catholic bishops was able to bring both sides to an agreement, thus ending the strike.

Chavez went on a hunger strike during the summer of 1968. He was protesting the

> The union that Cesar Chavez in 1962 started became part of the AFL-CIO, a powerful national labor organization, in 1966. Today the union is known as the United Farm Workers of America.

use of *pesticides* by California table-grape growers. He said the pesticides were dangerous to the farm workers because they could cause cancer. By bringing people's attention to this problem, Chavez was successful in getting 26 major growers to sign a contract with the union agreeing to better working conditions and fair pay.

Cesar Chavez not only helped the migrant workers, but his efforts went far to improve the lives of all Mexican Americans. His work through media appearances and interviews, hunger strikes and well-organized *boycotts* brought the poor conditions to the attention of the country. His pictures and descriptions let all Americans know how Mexican Americans were often treated. ✵

A Mexican family makes a run for the border from Tijuana, Mexico, to San Diego, California. This border region is the busiest in the country. Many immigrants from Mexico and Central America, both legal and illegal, pass through this area hoping to find a better life in the United States.

4

Personal Immigration Stories

German and Irma Pantoja have lived in Indiana for several years. German came from Uriangato. This city is found in the state of Guanajuato in south central Mexico. It was here that he learned how to bake Mexican breads and pastries.

It was difficult for German to make a living. He talked with some friends, and they decided to see if they could find a better life in the United States. German first worked in the fields around Marion, Indiana. Then he heard about *foundry* work available in a small northern town in Indiana. It was while he was working at the foundry that he met Irma, who later became his wife.

To make extra money, German and Irma started making bread and cookies in their home and selling them. In December 2000, a long-time dream came true when they opened a *panaderia* (bakery). "We started to make breads here and the people liked them," said Irma. "They began asking for them, so now we have a business."

German's business began with a small Kitchen Aid mixer. When the demand became greater, he bought a larger Hobart mixer. "Now I have a large 60 core mixer," he says. "Someday I will buy one even larger." Some of the cookies are shaped like a moon and have smaller cookies inside. One of their most popular breads is called *Campechana*.

German and Irma are in their bakery by 7:00 A.M. Their workday lasts until 8 P.M. It is a long day, and most of the time they are standing. But when asked how they feel about those long days, Irma says, "I've never had my own business. This seemed like something impossible, but little by little, we are doing it. We are making a living together."

This is true in many cases. In Fort Wayne, Indiana alone, the Hispanic population has gone from 4,679 in 1990 to 17,212 in 2006. Hispanics make up 5.1 percent of the city's total population.

In Florida, the numbers are even greater. According to the 2006 American Community Survey, Hispanics now make up 20.1 percent of Florida's population. This number represents 3.6 million residents. In fact, Hispanics have passed African Americans to become Florida's largest minority group.

A Census Bureau report also estimates that, combined, the Chicago and Los Angeles metropolitan areas and the state of Texas are home to more than half of the United States' Mexican-born population.

Raymond Ramirez was born April 4, 1921, in Monterrey, Mexico. He migrated with his family in 1925. At the time the family went north, migrating to American was a simple matter of paying a tax. "You paid *diez centavos* (10 cents) [. . .], came over here, and started working wherever you could,' Ramirez recalls. "We settled in Calvert, Texas. I went to school there for four years, and my father started farming."

The family had only one mattress to sleep on. They huddled together and used old clothes for covers. Sometimes they were able to get blankets from the farmers.

German Pantoja prepares rolls in his Fort Wayne, Indiana, bakery. Opening the bakery was a dream come true for German and his wife Irma, who emigrated from Mexico.

Raymond's father could play the bugle. He had volunteered with Pancho Villa to be his bugler. Raymond enjoyed listening to his father tell stories about his adventures riding with Pancho Villa.

When World War II began, Raymond volunteered and was sent to England. "That's where I got my citizenship papers," he proudly says.

Inner tubes drift ashore on the New River downstream from the U.S.–Mexico border near Calexico, California. As many as 100 people per night float down the highly contaminated river in an attempt to enter the United States.

"My children are grown now, seven sons and one daughter. My wife and I always taught them to work hard, put a little money in the bank, and forget about it. Just keep puttin' it in. And if you need a little more money, do a little extra work. That's what I've been doing all my life."

Joe Alvarez's grandfather came across the border illegally during the early days of immigration. He worked and then took the money home to the family.

After his grandparents had passed away, Joe's father and mother left Durango, Mexico, in the early 1940s. The poverty was so bad they could hardly make a living.

Joe was born in 1950 on a farm in Ramonville, Texas. He was one of 14 children. They picked watermelons, oranges, and grapefruit. Joe's father also worked on the tractor. The family raised chickens for meat and eggs.

When Joe was about six, the family began moving from place to place following the crops. They picked tomatoes and cucumbers. They hoed potatoes and beets. It was hard work. Joe began working in the fields when he was only nine years old.

Life in the migrant camps could be rough. There was a lot of violence. There was no normal routine. Many of the fathers were drinkers. Joe thought that his life would be just like the other migrants—working and moving.

In 1963, however, his family settled in Van Wert, Ohio. Joe said, "We pulled in the drive and there was only one house. The farmer

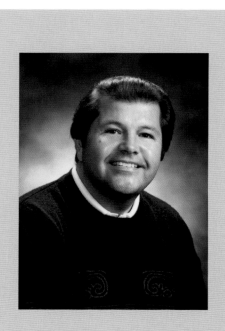

Like many hardworking Mexican Americans, Joe Alvarez has tried to give something back to the community where he found success. As a sheriff, he has helped local communities establish programs to reduce crime.

gave us his big barn to live in. We strung wires and hung blankets so we even had rooms." That was one of the nicest places his family had ever lived.

Joe was now able to go to school regularly. He was the first in his family to graduate from high school and then went on to college. Joe moved to Fort Wayne, Indiana, and met his wife while in college. He worked in a juvenile detention facility because he wanted to help people. Hearing that there were openings in the Fort Wayne Sheriff's Department, Joe applied and was accepted.

Now, more than 30 years later, Joe Alvarez is in charge of the Crime Stoppers Program in Fort Wayne, and has helped other communities develop this same program. He truly lives to help others and give back the good things that have been given to him.

The stories of German and Irma, Raymond, and Joe are just a few of the many success stories of Mexican-American immigrants who have found their niche in American society. These are people who were determined to come to the United States, work hard, and create a better life for themselves and their families. ✴

Richard Ochoa waits on a customer at his restaurant, La Margarita. Richard, whose story was told in the first chapter of this book, is a second-generation American whose parents came from Mexico during the 1920s.

43

A teenage girl wearing a dancing dress tries on a sombrero at a festival in Austin, Texas. Many immigrants try to fit in by absorbing American culture, but some find it is just as important to embrace their ethnic traditions as well.

5 Immigration Today

During the 1950's, immigration from Mexico doubled from 5.9 percent of the total number of immigrants to the United States to 11.9 percent. In the 1960s, it went up to 13.3 percent of the total.

In 1951 the Bracero Program was formalized as the Mexican Farm Labor Supply Program and the Mexican Labor Agreement. The program brought about 350,000 Mexican workers to the United States until it ended in 1964.

However, during the 1950s the U.S. government also took steps to restrict immigration from Mexico. In 1952 Congress passed the Immigration and Nationality Act of 1952. It maintained a limit on immigration from certain countries, including Mexico. The U.S. also cracked down on illegal immigrants living in the country. From 1954 to 1958, immigration officials conducted an operation to send illegal immigrants back to Mexico. More than 3.8 million persons of Mexican descent were *deported*. Only a few had deportation hearings. Thousands of legitimate Mexican Americans were also arrested and detained until they could prove that they were legal citizens of the United States.

In 1964 Congress passed the Civil Rights Act. This prohibited discrimination on the basis of gender, creed, race, or ethnic background. Although this new law was created as part of the black civil rights movement, it also meant that Mexican Americans could not be discriminated against in advertising, recruitment, hiring, job classification, promotions, discharge, wages and salaries and other terms of employment. The Equal Employment Opportunity Commission was established to monitor job discrimination.

After immigration restrictions were lifted in 1965, experienced farm laborers began to encourage other Mexicans to move to the United States to work.

By 1970, 82 percent of the Hispanic population of the nation lived in nine states. That number had increased to 90 percent by 1990. The most popular states were California, Texas, New York, Florida, Illinois and New Jersey.

Unfortunately, between the years of 1978 and 1988 many Hispanic children lived in poverty. By 1989, 38 percent of Hispanic children fit into the poverty level.

The 1980's saw immigration rise sharply. Legal immigration surpassed 1.6 million. Millions of Mexican immigrants were granted permanent residences. By 1989, immigration from Latin America had risen from 44.3 percent to 61.4 percent of total immigration to the United States. Mexico accounted for 37.1 percent of Latin American immigrants to the United States.

At the start of the new millennium, Hispanics are the fastest-growing ethnic group in the United States. According to the 2006 American Community Survey, there were more than 44.2 million Americans of Hispanic or Latino descent living in the country. Of this group,

The North American Free Trade Agreement (NAFTA) was signed into existence in 1992 by representatives from Mexico, the United States, and Canada. The legislation, which went into effect in 1994, has given Mexico's economy a boost by easing restrictions on the production of goods.

The United States Citizenship and Immigration Services (USCIS) is an agency that is part of the U.S. Department of Homeland Security. USCIS was created in 2003 to replace the U.S. Immigration and Naturalization Service (INS). Citizenship and Immigration Services oversees the immigration and naturalization of people who wish to enter the United States. The agency reviews applications from prospective immigrants, and conducts hearings to decide whether immigrants can become U.S. citizens.

Another agency that is part of the Department of Homeland Security is responsible for border control and preventing illegal immigration. This is U.S. Immigration and Customs Enforcement (ICE). A branch of ICE, the Office of Detention and Removal, is responsible for enforcing the nation's immigration laws and deporting illegal immigrants.

Mexican-Americans make up the largest majority, about 64 percent. There were more than 28.3 million American citizens of Mexican descent registered in the census that year.

Education is still one of the biggest problems facing the Mexican-American community. Only 56 percent of Hispanics have graduated from high school. Part of this may be due to the language problem. Many Mexican children hear only Spanish spoken at home and do not learn the English language.

Schools are striving to correct this problem. Spanish-speaking teachers and counselors are being hired in schools across the nation. In some areas, both Spanish and English are required subjects.

A tourist looks through a display of clothing at a market in Ensenada, Baja California, Mexico. While millions of Mexicans immigrate to the United States each year, large numbers of American shoppers and tourists travel south across the border to visit Mexico.

President George W. Bush pledges allegiance to the flag after a ceremony on Ellis Island in 2001. Bush was promoting his administration's plans for reforming the Immigration and Naturalization Service.

One thing that has changed the relationship between the United States and Mexico has been the North American Free Trade Agreement (NAFTA). This is an agreement between Mexico, Canada, and the United States. NAFTA created a free-trade zone among the three nations, setting standards for minimum wages, working conditions, and environmental protection.

NAFTA has created new jobs in Mexico, and more opportunities for the people there. More industry has developed in the border towns. NAFTA has given smaller businesses an opportunity to grow and expand.

However, there are still problems. Even with all this industry, there are not enough jobs in the country, so many Mexicans still cross the border to look for work and a better life in the United States. ✷

Famous Mexican Americans

Romana Acosta Banuelos served as Treasurer of the United States from 1971 to 1974 under President Richard M. Nixon. She was the first Mexican-American woman to hold such a high government position. She also founded the Pan American National Bank of East Los Angeles. It is the first bank owned and operated by Mexican Americans.

Philip Arreola, the Chief of Police in Milwaukee, has received many awards, including the Detroit Police Department Medal of Valor in 1986, 11 merit citations, 20 commendations and two chief's merit awards.

Joan Baez is a professional folk singer and political activist.

Vikki Carr is a famous singer. In 1989, her album *Esos Hombres* won gold records in Mexico, Chile, Puerto Rico, and the United States. Today she is active in scholarships that provide higher education to Mexican-American youths.

Denise Chavez writes stories, plays and poems. In 1988, she became a professor in the Drama Department of the University of Houston.

Oscar De La Hoya is a professional boxer who won ten world championship belts in six different weight classes. He also owns a sports promotion company, Golden Boy Promotions.

Archbishop Patrick F. Flores has received many honors for programs he began in the church and in government on behalf of the civil rights of Hispanics and immigrants. In 1986, he was awarded the Medal of Freedom (Ellis Island Medal of Honor) in honor of the Statue of Liberty's 100th birthday.

Salma Hayek is an award-winning actress. She has also been successful as a film director, and as a television and film producer.

Nancy Lopez was a golfer who won the New Mexico Women's Open when she was only 12. In 1985, she won five tournaments and finished in the top 10 in 21 others.

Ellen Ochoa was the first Mexican-American woman to become an astronaut. She first flew in space aboard the shuttle *Discovery* in 1993.

Anthony Quinn was a film star in more than 100 movies. He won two Oscars and several Academy Award nominations. He helped produce the documentary, *The Voice of La Raza,* which addressed the problems of Mexican Americans in the United States.

Bill Richardson was elected governor of New Mexico in 2003. He previously served as U.S. Secretary of Energy (1998-2001) in President Bill Clinton's cabinet, and was the U.S. Ambassador to the United Nations (1997-1998).

Ken Salazar is a U.S. Senator who represents the state of Colorado.

Lee Trevino was another famous golfer. He was the first player in history to shoot all four rounds of the United States Open under par.

Chronology

1951 The Bracero Program is formalized as the Mexican Farm Labor Supply Program and the Mexican Labor Agreement.

1952 Congress passes the Immigration and Nationality Act of 1952, imposing a limit on immigration from particular countries.

1954–1958 3.8 million persons of Mexican descent are deported.

1962 Cesar Chavez organizes the United Farm Workers Organizing Committee in California.

1964 Congress passes the Civil Rights Act prohibiting discrimination on the basis of gender, creed, race, or ethnic background.

1965 Experienced braceros (farm laborers) encourage other Mexicans to immigrate to the United States to work not only in the agricultural areas but also in railroad camps.

1970 Eighty-two percent of the Hispanic population of the nation lives in nine states. That will number increase to 90 percent by 1990.

1994 The North American Free Trade Agreement (NAFTA) between Mexico, United States, and Canada goes into effect.

2000 More than 350,000 Mexicans immigrate legally to the United States.

2001 Mexican President Vicente Fox meets with U.S. President George W. Bush to discuss many issues, one of which is immigration (both legal and illegal) between their two countries.

2006 The American Community Survey reports that 28.3 million Americans are of Mexican descent.

2008 Hispanics remain the fastest-growing segment of the U.S. population, and Mexican Americans make up more than half of the Hispanic population in the United States.

An ancient Mayan carving stands guard near the El Castillo pyramid at Chichén Itzá, Yucatán. The Maya were one of several ancient civilizations that flourished in Mexico more than a thousand years ago. Today Mayan ruins such as this are popular tourist attractions.

Barrio Mexican neighborhood.

Boycott to stop or to refuse dealing with something such as an organization or company as a protest against it and to force it to change.

Bracero Mexican farm worker.

Deport to force someone to leave a country, usually to return to his or her country of origin.

Detention the act of keeping somebody in custody.

Discrimination unfair treatment of a person or group because of race, ethnic group, religion, or gender.

Drafting the art of making detailed plans or drawings of buildings, ships, aircraft, or machines.

Foundry a building where the shaping of glass or metal is done.

Green card an identity card and work permit issued in the United States to people from other countries.

Liberal someone who favors tolerance or reform, especially with regard to politics.

Mestizo a person who has parents of both Native American and European ancestry.

Opposition a resistant viewpoint against something.

Pesticide a chemical substance used to kill pests, primarily insects.

Plateau a hill or mountain with a level top.

Rally to come together for a common purpose or a common cause.

Revolution the overthrow of a ruler or political system.

Vigilante someone who punishes lawbreakers personally and illegally instead of relying on legal authorities.

Further Reading

Baughan, Brian. *Cesar Chavez*. Philadelphia: Mason Crest Publishers, 2009.

Caravantes, Ernesto R. *The Mexican American Mind*. Lanham, MD: Hamilton Books, 2008.

Marcovitz, Hal. *Mexican Americans*. Philadelphia: Mason Crest Publishers, 2009.

Martinez, Glenn A. *Mexican Americans and Language: Del dicho al hecho*. Tuscon: University of Arizona Press, 2006.

Schroeder, Michael. *Mexican Americans*. New York: Chelsea House, 2006.

West, John. *Mexican American Folklore*. Atlanta: August House, 2007.

Tracing Your Mexican-American Ancestors

Beers, Henry Putney. *Spanish and Mexican Records of the American Southwest*. Tuscon: University of Arizona Press, 1979.

Carmack, Sharon DeBartolo. *A Genealogist's Guide to Discovering Your Immigrant and Ethnic Ancestors*. Cincinnati: Betterway Books, 2000.

Guide to Spanish and Mexican Land Grants in South Texas. Austin, Texas: General Land Office, 1988.

Internet Resources

http://www.census.gov

The official Web site of the U.S. Bureau of the Census contains information about the most recent census taken in 2000.

http://www.mexicanamericans.com/

A site dedicated to educating the American public about Mexican Americans, past and present, their history, traditions, and culture.

http://www.malc.org/

A non-profit, non-partisan organization, the Mexican American Legislative Caucus works with the Texas government to ensure Latinos across the state receive the support and recognition needed for issues and concerns they, as a continually growing economic and political sector, face.

http://mallfoundation.org/

The non-profit Mexican American Legislative Leadership Foundation works with Latino youth to develop a professional understanding of government, while encouraging civic participation.

http://www.californiahistory.net/

The history of California, including timelines, images, etc., created by the California Historical Society.

http://www.univision.net/corp/en/index.jsp

Univision is the largest Spanish language media company serving the United States Hispanic population.

Immigration Figures

Mexican Immigrants Obtaining U.S. Citizenship, by Decade

1820–29:	3,855
1830–39:	7,187
1840–49:	3,069
1850–59:	3,446
1860–69:	1,957
1870–79:	5,133
1880–89:	2,405*
1890–99:	734*
1900–09:	31,188
1910–19:	185,334
1920–29:	498,945
1930–39:	32,709
1940–49:	56,158
1950–59:	273,847
1960–69:	441,824
1970–79:	621,218
1980–89:	1,009,586
1990–99:	2,757,418
2000–07	1,352,084

*Incomplete data available.

Source: Yearbook of Immigration Statistics, 2007.

Index

Photo Credits

Contributors

Barry Moreno has been librarian and historian at the Ellis Island Immigration Museum and the Statue of Liberty National Monument since 1988. He is the author of *The Statue of Liberty Encyclopedia*, which was published by Simon & Schuster in October 2000. He is a native of Los Angeles, California. After graduation from California State University at Los Angeles, where he earned a degree in history, he joined the National Park Service as a seasonal park ranger at the Statue of Liberty; he eventually became the monument's librarian. In his spare time, Barry enjoys reading, writing, and studying foreign languages and grammar. His biography has been included in *Who's Who Among Hispanic Americans, The Directory of National Park Service Historians, Who's Who in America,* and *The Directory of American Scholars.*

Linda R. Wade is a retired school librarian. She served 23 years in the same school she attended as a child. She has taught writing, both locally and at national writing conferences, for several years. She received her education from Olivet Nazarene University and Indiana University, as well as from numerous writing conferences. This is Mrs. Wade's 28th book since 1989. In her free time, she enjoys crafts as well as reading and writing at the lake. She and her husband, Edward, travel across the United States visiting their children, historic places, and national parks.